WRONG TIME, WRONG PLACE

Simon Kernick

SHORTLIST

First published in 2013
by Arrow Books
This Large Print edition published
2013 by AudioGO Ltd
by arrangement with
Random House Group Limited

ISBN 978 1 4713 3386 6

British Library Cataloguing in Publication Data available

Printed and bound in Great Britain
by MPG Books Group Limited

CHAPTER ONE

It had been two nights since she had heard Eva's screams as they took her away. Now there was only silence, which meant her friend was dead.

Tara knew they'd be coming for her next. It was that simple. That was why she was here. To die. She had no idea what she was meant to have done to deserve this fate. It was all like some strange nightmare.

One night—a week, two weeks ago?—Tara had gone to sleep in the filthy little room she called home, with the constant drone of the buses going past outside the window. Then, when she'd woken up, she was here in this tiny, windowless cell. She was naked, with only a blanket for warmth, and chained to the wall by her ankle, like some kind of beaten animal.

At first she'd thought she was

completely alone in the stony silence, and she'd started crying with despair. But then she'd heard a voice speaking her language—Albanian—from beyond the wall, asking her name. It was her friend Eva, and she was being held in the cell next door.

Eva had told her that the same thing had happened to both of them, and not just the kidnapping. Like Tara, she'd been talked into coming to England by a man who'd promised her a good job and a release from the poverty she knew at home, only to force her to work in a brothel as a virtual slave. They even both came from the same area of Kosovo.

In their cells, Tara and Eva had talked every day for hours and hours at a time. About home and family, about their hopes and dreams, about what they'd do if they ever got out of there (Eva wanted to go to Paris and climb the Eiffel Tower, Tara wanted to learn to ride a horse).

But now Tara was alone with

2

only the constant, dead silence for company.

That didn't mean she'd given up, though. No, if anything, what had happened to Eva had filled her with a new energy. Tara was going to escape. And she had a plan.

There was a piece of loose brick in the wall behind where she sat. She'd found it on her first day here. Ever since then she'd been working to get it free, wearing her nails down as she dug out the mortar on either side of it, until finally she was able to twist and pull at it, slowly loosening it.

Now she was holding a solid half-brick in her hand. It would be a useful weapon, if only she had the physical strength, and the chance, to use it properly.

Tara had never seen the man who held her prisoner. She was always made to turn round and face the wall on those few times when he came in to change the bucket she used as a toilet. He gave the order in Albanian but in a thick accent she didn't recognise, and it sounded like they were the only words in Albanian he knew.

Twice a day, he pushed a plate of food and a plastic bottle of water through a flap in the cell door. He always wore black gloves, but sometimes his sleeve rode up and she could see the thick hair on his arms, and the swirling shape of a tattoo on his skin.

She could hear him now, moving about outside the door. She tucked the brick behind her, scared but hopeful too that he'd come in, knowing this was probably the best chance she was going to get.

But then she saw the flap opening. He wasn't going to come inside.

Usually she put the blanket over herself when she heard him coming, but this time she threw it off, letting out a low, painful moan, trying to sound as if she was sick. At the same time she rubbed her stomach and pulled a face. There was a spyhole in the cell door, and she knew he'd be looking through it, checking her out.

He probably wouldn't care at all if she was ill, but if he saw her naked, it might be enough to get him interested. Her naked body had certainly interested all the other men she'd been forced to entertain these past few months.

She moaned again, louder and longer this time. The flap closed without the food being pushed through.

The key turned in the lock and he stepped inside. He was tall and dressed in black. A hood covered his head, like some kind of hangman from the history books Tara had read as a child. The man frightened her. God, how he frightened her. His arms were thick and she could imagine him using them to throttle the life out of his victims.

'Be strong,' she told herself as she writhed around on the floor, acting like she was dying. All the time she could hear her heart beating in her chest, as the fear pumped through her.

He was coming over. Bending down, saying something she didn't understand. Looking at her with suspicion in his eyes.

She could feel the brick in the small of her back. She rolled over, still moaning, her arm dropping out of sight, knowing this was it. Her chance.

He grabbed her by the hair and pulled her round so she was facing him. 'Bitch,' he said. It was a word she recognised, because it was used so often by the men in the brothel.

Then something changed in his eyes. Anger was replaced by lust, and she felt him roughly pulling her legs apart with a gloved hand, making weird moaning noises beneath his mask.

That was the moment she grabbed the brick, sat up suddenly, and hit him on the side of the head.

'Bitch!' he howled a second time, his voice echoing around the tiny cell. He grabbed the hand holding the brick by the wrist, yanking it back painfully, his eyes burning with fury.

Knowing she couldn't afford to stop now, Tara kept up her attack, jabbing her forefinger into his left eye like a knife, feeling its soft fleshiness give way.

This time he screamed in real pain, trying to twist his head away. At the same time, he relaxed his grip on her wrist.

She pulled her arm free and struggled out from under him. The chain securing her ankle to the wall rattled angrily as she jumped to her feet. She hit him for a second time as he swayed on his knees, yelping in pain.

The brick shattered into a dozen pieces, and for a moment Tara thought she'd failed. Her heart sank, but then the man grunted and fell on to his side, barely moving.

Feeling a rush of excitement, she crouched down beside him and pulled the set of keys from his belt, praying that one would unlock the chain around her ankle.

There must have been a dozen keys of various shapes and sizes, and the first one didn't fit. Nor did the second.

The guard was beginning to come round. He let out a moan, and one arm moved.

Tara tried a third key, her hands shaking so much she could barely put it into the slot. Another wrong one.

He was turning round now, one hand still over his injured eye, but the other one staring at her.

Come on, come on.

She tried a fourth key. It didn't work.

The man reached round behind his back. When his hand came back into view, Tara gasped and panic swept through her. He was holding a huge knife with a jagged blade. She'd seen hunters using knives like that to gut deer back in Kosovo.

Willing herself to stay calm, trying desperately to forget that in the next few seconds she could die, Tara tried another key. She slipped it into the lock with shaking hands. The lock clicked, and the metal clamp that had been painfully attached to her from the moment she'd first woken up in this place opened. Just at that moment, the guard lunged towards her with the knife. She jumped backwards, hitting the wall behind her. The tip of the blade came so close to her belly that she could almost feel it touching her.

But with the chain removed from her, she suddenly felt a new surge of energy. Taking advantage of the fact that her attacker was still on his knees, she darted around him and leaped at the cell door. She flung it open and ran into the narrow, dimly-lit corridor outside.

Tara had no idea where she was going but she could tell she was in some kind of basement area. The walls and floors were the same cold stone as the cell, the only light provided by a single bulb hanging down from the ceiling.

To her right was a flight of steps, and she sprinted towards them. Her legs were stiff from lack of exercise, but sheer terror and a strong desire to live drove her on. She passed other cell doors, making her wonder how many girls had been locked in this horrible place, and then she was up the steps, taking them two at a time.

She could hear him chasing behind her, his footsteps heavy on the stone, the curses raging in his throat.

There was a door at the top, and she prayed it wouldn't be locked. Grabbing the handle, she gave it a yank so hard that when it opened it almost knocked her back down the steps.

She charged through the gap, then screamed in despair. She was suddenly in a dark, empty cupboard with a blank wall directly in front of her, and no obvious way out. She hammered on the wall, still screaming, but it wasn't doing any good. Nothing budged. She was trapped, and her attacker was almost at the top of the steps.

Turning round, she kicked at the door with all her strength, the force of the kick sending it flying into him. He let out a yelp and stumbled backwards. At the same time, Tara lost her balance and fell backwards herself in the opposite direction.

She must have hit some sort of lever that opened a trap door, because suddenly the wall wasn't there any more and she was rolling onto a thick carpet in a grand-looking living room with expensive furnishings. Daylight was glaring in through huge windows, making her squint with pain.

Tara was straight up on her feet, sprinting out of the room and down an equally grand hallway with dozens of incredible animal heads lining the walls. This was the house of a very rich person, but all she could think of was getting out.

There was another door ahead. It looked like the front door to the house. Behind her, she could hear her jailer calling someone. There was increasing alarm in his voice, as if he knew he'd made a terrible mistake. The next second, Tara was outside, the fresh air hitting her in the face like a slap. All she could see in the distance was trees.

Trees and freedom.

CHAPTER TWO

'All there is up here is bloody trees,' said Guy, sounding knackered and pissed off. 'I hope you two know

12

where you're going, because I don't.'

'Course we do,' said Ash, trying to keep the annoyance out of her voice.

The weekend was only a few hours old and yet she was already bitterly regretting coming away on a walking trip with Guy and Tracy. It wasn't that they were bad people—they weren't—but they were Nick's friends rather than hers (Nick and Guy had gone to university together). And they both had this hugely irritating habit of talking about how much fun they had living in Singapore, where Guy earned squillions and paid only 10 per cent tax, and Tracy lived a relaxed expat lifestyle. This seemed to consist solely of tennis, drinks parties and luxury treatments, but despite Tracy's best efforts at bigging it up, it sounded to Ash as much fun as having your teeth pulled out.

'I don't miss this country, you know,' continued Guy as the four of them walked down a slight incline towards a pine forest that led to the lodge they'd booked. 'You pay all these taxes and what do you get for your money? Sod all.'

Ash and Nick, who were walking a few yards ahead, exchanged glances, and Nick raised an eyebrow. It was clear to Ash that he wasn't having the time of his life either.

'Well, you get views like this,' said Nick, stopping and looking back down the hill they'd just climbed to the forest-covered valley below, where a river wound away gently into the distance. 'I bet you don't see many sights like that in Singapore.'

'That's true,' said Tracy, who'd been banging on less than her husband about the joys of their new home. 'It is beautiful.' She closed her eyes, basking in the last rays of the early evening sun, looking like she was enjoying herself for the first time that day.

Guy wasn't convinced. 'Lombok in Indonesia is just as beautiful. And a lot warmer too. We're thinking about buying a holiday home there.'

'I don't know about you lot, but I could murder a pint right now,' said Nick, trying to change the subject.

'I concur,' said Guy, who liked using big words where little ones would do. 'Is there a pub round here anywhere?'

'Afraid not,' said Ash. 'I did say the lodge was in the middle of nowhere when I booked it.'

Guy looked annoyed. 'You weren't lying.'

God knows what they were going to do tomorrow, thought Ash. Or Sunday. They'd come to this isolated part of Scotland to walk. It was something the four of them had done together a couple of times before. But as Ash thought back to those weekends now, she remembered that actually they'd been more about sitting around drinking, smoking dope and having a natter rather than going for proper all-day hikes.

She and Nick had changed since those days. They appreciated the great outdoors for what it was—a much-needed escape from the grim routine of London life. It was clear that Guy and Tracy didn't feel the same way, although at least Tracy was making an effort.

'Who the hell is that?' said Nick, as they all turned round, following his gaze.

At first, Ash couldn't see what he was looking at, then she saw someone running towards them through long grass about a hundred metres away. It looked like whoever it was had just come out of the line of pine trees along the ridge above them, and they were clearly in a real hurry.

'Is she *naked*?' asked Guy, sounding genuinely interested in something for the first time that day.

'Jesus, she is,' said Nick. 'I wonder if she's all right.'

The girl was indeed naked, and

young too, with a thin spindly body and long blonde hair. She was coming towards them at a sprint, stumbling as she went. Instinctively the four of them started towards her.

*   *   *

Tara was exhausted, and panting so hard she could hardly breathe. She sprinted towards the four people with the packs on their backs. They looked like hikers. They could help her. Take her somewhere warm and give her something to eat. After that, she didn't care. She just wanted to go home. Back to her family.

She'd been running for a long time now. Her feet were torn and cut, and her body was covered in scratches. Thankfully there was no sign of the man who'd been following her. She'd outrun the bastard.

As she reached the group of hikers, she collapsed to her knees, unable to continue any further. Tears rolled down her face.

It was hard to believe but, for the first time since she'd come to this terrible country, she was actually free.

*   *   *

'It's OK,' said Ash, crouching down beside the girl. 'We're here now. What's happened?'

In between sobs, the girl said something in a foreign language that sounded Eastern European.

'I think she might be Polish,' said Guy.

'What happened to you?' asked Tracy, putting an arm round the girl's shoulders.

The girl flinched.

'OK, let's give her some space,' said Ash, taking off her jacket and giving it to the girl so she didn't have to sit there stark naked. 'It's obvious she's had a bad experience.'

She stood back up, noticing that

the girl had a vivid red mark round one ankle where the skin had rubbed away. It looked like she'd been shackled or something. Nervously, Ash looked up towards the line of trees, wondering what had happened to the girl in there.

'Can you speak any English?' she asked the girl as gently as possible, using all the skills she'd learned in her job as a primary school teacher to put her at ease.

The girl shook her head, wiped her eyes, then suddenly pointed back towards the trees.

'Do you think she's been raped?' asked Guy.

Tracy gave him a look. 'Guy . . . don't say that.'

'I'm just asking.'

Ash tensed. 'Something bad's happened to her. I think she was being chased.'

'There doesn't look like there's anyone chasing her,' said Tracy.

'Either way, we need to get an

19

ambulance. She's been through a trauma.'

'I'll phone one,' said Nick, taking out his mobile, then almost immediately cursing. 'There's no reception up here.'

Ash checked her own phone, as did Guy and Tracy, all with the same result. One of the reasons Ash had chosen this place was its remoteness. Nick was always getting out-of-hours calls from work, and she'd wanted this weekend to be different, so she'd been happy to be somewhere where his phone wasn't going to ring constantly. Now she realised just how far they were from any sort of help.

'Jesus, what the hell's wrong with this country?' grunted Guy, staring with disgust at his phone. 'I can get perfect reception in any Third World hellhole, yet here—'

'Shut up, Guy,' Nick snapped. 'We don't need your moaning now, all right?'

'There's a landline at the lodge,'

said Ash, 'and it's only ten minutes away. We'll call an ambulance from there, and if we have to, we'll drive her to a hospital.'

'But we don't even know who she is,' said Tracy, sounding as put out as her husband.

'Exactly. And she can't tell us. So we need to help her.' Jesus, thought Ash. What was wrong with these people? Had their time abroad sucked out all their humanity?

She put a hand out to the girl and helped her to her feet. As she did so she noticed something on her wrist. It looked like a plain black wristband, but it had a hard plastic casing and was an extremely tight fit.

The girl seemed to notice it too, almost for the first time. She tried to take it off, but it wouldn't budge.

'What do you reckon this is?' Ash asked her husband, showing him the wristband.

They both examined it.

'I don't know,' said Nick. 'It just

looks like a bangle.'

'Except it's locked on to her wrist.'

The girl pulled her arm away, tapped her finger on the wristband and then pointed back towards the trees. There was fear in her eyes.

'I don't like this,' said Tracy.

Guy put an arm round her. 'Me neither. If we're going to hang on to her, then let's get going before it gets dark.'

The sun was dropping behind the opposite hill and the air was feeling colder.

As one, the group turned and started walking towards the lodge, the girl moving faster than any of them, and every now and then looking back over her shoulder.

*   *   *

He watched them go from his position a hundred metres away, and cursed. He'd almost had the little bitch earlier. It had been easy enough to track her progress using the GPS clamped to her wrist. He thought he'd cut her off, but she'd been faster than he expected. She had the kind of stamina that he wouldn't have thought possible in someone who'd just spent the last two weeks chained in a cellar. Then again, as he knew all too well, desperation does strange things to a person.

Now, though, he had a real problem.

They all did.

CHAPTER THREE

'Let's get the poor thing some clothes, she's freezing,' said Ash as she unlocked the door to the lodge and stepped inside. 'Come on, sit down.' She led the girl over to the sofa.

The girl sat down, grabbed a

cushion and hugged it. She looked terrified.

Ash gave her a reassuring smile. 'It's OK. You're safe now. Do you have a name?' she said slowly. 'What is your name?'

The girl just shook her head and looked away.

'She can have some of my clothes,' said Tracy. 'I packed a load of things.'

'Trace, are you sure?' whined Guy.

'Course I am. Jesus, Guy. Look at her shivering. Have some heart.'

Tracy ran upstairs to her suitcase while Guy stared after her. Ash was pleased to see the look of shock on his face. The man could be a real idiot at times. She wondered what her husband had ever seen in him.

'We've got a problem,' said Nick from the corner of the room where he was holding the landline phone to his ear.

Ash felt her chest tighten. 'What is it?'

'The bloody phone's out of order.'

'We'll have to drive her to the nearest hospital.'

'Jesus,' sighed Guy. 'That's all we need.'

'Look, I don't want to have to do it either, Guy,' said Ash, turning on him, 'but we haven't got any bloody choice.'

'What is it?' said Tracy, coming back down the stairs with a pair of tracksuit bottoms and a garish pink hoodie. She handed them to Ash, who'd clearly been chosen as their main contact with the girl.

'The landline isn't working either,' Guy told her.

'You two don't have to worry,' said Nick. 'Ash and I will take her. There's booze in the fridge. You just stay here until we get back. We'll try not to be too long.'

Guy nodded. He and Tracy both looked relieved, having been let off the hook.

Ash handed the girl the clothes.

'Put these on. We're going to take you to the doctor now.' She spoke slowly and carefully, as if this would somehow help the girl understand her.

The girl nodded silently and put on the clothes.

'All right, let's go,' said Nick, grabbing the keys to their Land Rover.

Gently, Ash lifted the girl to her feet and together they followed Nick out of the front door.

It was nearly dark and the wind was picking up, sweeping through the trees that surrounded the lodge on every side. When they'd arrived that morning in the sunshine, Ash had thought it was a perfect location, far from the city crowds. But now that this mysterious girl had arrived out of the blue, naked and bruised, it had suddenly taken on a more menacing air. Something had happened to her out in these woods, something terrible, and Ash was suddenly glad that they were leaving.

She got in the back with the girl, putting a protective arm round her shoulders, while Nick started the engine and pulled away in a crunch of gravel.

Almost immediately the car seemed uncontrollable. Nick turned the steering wheel, trying to right it, but the car seemed to have a mind of its own. It bumped up and down as if it was being shaken. Nick brought the car to a stop and pulled up the handbrake.

'What is it?' Ash asked him.

Nick didn't answer. Instead he got out, took a quick look round the car, then pulled open the back door. His expression was grim. 'Let's get back in the house. Now.'

He grabbed Ash by the arm. In normal circumstances, she'd have yelled at him to let go of her. Ash didn't like being manhandled by anyone. But these weren't normal circumstances. Nick looked scared,

27

and that scared Ash, because usually he was the calmest person she knew. It was why he was such a damn good lawyer.

'What's going on?' she said, pulling the girl out with her.

'Someone's slashed the tyres,' he hissed, leading the two of them back to the lodge, his fingers shaking as he unlocked the front door.

Ash risked a look over her shoulder, and immediately saw the gaping tears in each of the nearside tyres. The girl looked too, and let out a frightened, animal-like whimper.

Guy and Tracy had already sat down on the sofa with the TV on. They both jumped up like guilty teenagers caught groping each other when the others came back in.

'Everything all right?' asked Guy, looking past them to the girl.

'We've got a situation,' Nick told them, locking the door behind him and pulling the curtains as he explained what had happened.

'You mean, all four of the tyres have been slashed?' demanded Guy.

Nick nodded. 'All four of them. So it's deliberate.'

'But who'd do that?' asked Tracy, her voice rising several tones.

'I have no idea, but whoever it is clearly has a problem with us.'

Guy looked angry and put-out, like a spoilt child. 'Why? We haven't done anything to them. It must be something to do with her.' He pointed at the girl, who shrank away from his accusing stare. 'Whoever's after her knows she's with us. I say we let her go. It's her they want. We don't even have a clue who the hell it is who's after her. We don't even have a clue who she is.' He took a step towards the girl. 'Go on,' he shouted, 'get the hell out of here! Now!'

'Leave it!' shouted Nick, blocking Guy's way. 'It's not her fault.'

'It's not our fault either,' said Tracy. 'I'm really sorry but I'm with

Guy. She's not our problem. She should go.'

Ash felt her anger rising. 'You want to send a young girl out into the darkness alone, Tracy? Is that what you're saying?'

'We don't know what she's done. She might have really hurt someone, and they're looking for revenge. Otherwise why are they so keen to stop her leaving?'

'Bullshit. Look at her. The poor thing wouldn't say boo to a goose.'

'Then why's someone trying so hard to get her?' demanded Guy, trying to step past Nick. 'Come on, let's ask her. I bet she speaks English better than the rest of us.'

Nick put a hand on his friend's chest. 'Let's just calm down.'

But Guy had the bit between his teeth now and he tried to shove Nick out of the way, at the same time pointing an accusing finger at the girl. 'Come on, start bloody talking.'

Nick, though, was a lot bigger and

stronger than his friend and he easily held him back. He tried again to take the heat out of the situation with more calm words.

Ash looked at the girl. 'Don't worry,' she told her, giving her a reassuring smile, but it was already too late for that. The poor thing looked terrified. Like a rabbit caught in a car's headlights.

Then, without warning, she ran for the front door, unlocking it in one swift movement and dashing out into the night.

Instinctively, Ash chased after her, not thinking about the dangers that might lurk outside. The girl was quick, but so was Ash. She also had the advantage of wearing shoes on the gravel. She thrust out a hand and grabbed the girl by the hood of Tracy's top. 'Come on, it's all right,' she said, pulling the girl into a tight bearhug, trying desperately to make herself understood. 'No one's going to hurt you.'

She heard Nick coming up behind her. 'Ash, get back inside. Now.'

'I'm coming. I'm coming.'

Ash loosened her grip on the girl, which turned out to be a mistake. The girl immediately wriggled away from her, shoved Ash backwards and set off again at a run.

Ash went to follow but Nick grabbed her by the arm for the second time that night. 'Let her go,' he snapped.

Ash watched as the girl reached the end of the driveway, her battered feet crunching on the gravel, before being swallowed up by the woods. A part of Ash—the brave part—wanted to run after her and drag her back to where she'd be safe and warm. Another part kept her rooted to the spot. Jesus, the poor thing had to be terrified of something.

'We can't just leave her,' she told her husband. Even so, she didn't resist as Nick led her back inside.

Tara tore through the trees, telling herself that she wouldn't stop until she reached a town. She had no idea how far away one could be, or indeed where she even was. She assumed she must still be in England, but it was an England that was totally strange to her, a hilly wilderness where danger lurked at every turn. She'd thought the hikers would help her, and it had seemed like they were going to. The pretty dark-haired woman had been kind to her, but one of the other men had shouted and screamed. When she saw the slashed tyres on the car, she knew that her captor had somehow followed her to their house.

That was when she'd made the decision to run, not wanting to involve these people in what had happened to her. It wasn't fair. It wasn't their problem. So now, once again, Tara was on her own.

A three-quarter moon shone down, bathing the forest in eerie light. She didn't want light. She wanted darkness. Darkness would hide her. She looked round as she ran. The forest seemed empty, so she started to slow as the trees and bushes grew thicker, feeling the first sense of relief.

She glanced over her shoulder, saw no one following her, and turned back.

And ran straight into the knife.

Tara gasped as the blade was buried up to the hilt in her stomach, slicing through her flesh like it was slicing through a ripe orange. All her strength seemed to disappear in an instant.

Her attacker loomed up in front of her, an unmoving wall of black. She gazed into his cold, dark eyes as he withdrew the blade and drove it upwards into her heart, his gloved hand gripping her throat and holding her in place while she died.

CHAPTER FOUR

For a good minute, none of them spoke. Nick had locked the door and had the key in his hand. In the background, the TV was still blaring out some reality show rubbish, with lots of shouting and laughter.

Finally, Tracy broke the silence. 'Look, I didn't mean for her to go like that. But you know . . . I don't know what to do about this. I'm not used to this kind of drama.'

'None of us are, Tracy,' said Nick. 'I'm just a bloody lawyer, like Guy. The point is, we've got to deal with it.'

'For all we know she could have been the one who slashed the tyres,' said Guy.

'Don't be bloody daft,' snapped Ash, who was rapidly losing patience. 'Why on earth would she do that?'

'I don't know. But then I don't

know why any of this is bloody happening.'

Which, thought Ash, was a fair point. What had started out as a relaxing, if potentially dull, weekend trip had turned into a nightmare. Just like that.

Ash had been mugged once, a couple of years ago. Coming home to their flat late at night, she'd got out of the taxi and was walking towards the front door when a man had appeared from behind the gate post and punched her full in the face. There'd been no pain. Just total and utter shock. She'd stumbled backwards, putting a hand to her bleeding nose, and the man had simply pulled her handbag from her shoulder and run off up the street.

The whole thing had lasted a matter of seconds, but Ash would never forget that feeling of shock as the urban violence she'd read so much about, but had never actually seen, finally came crashing into her cosy world. She had that shocked, partly dazed feeling now. She felt she could understand a bit better Guy and Tracy's own reaction to the events that were happening around them.

'Maybe now she's gone, whoever slashed the tyres will leave us alone,' sighed Tracy, and any understanding Ash had felt for her disappeared.

'Jesus, don't you have any feelings for that poor girl?'

Nick put up a hand. 'Ash, leave it.'

'How can I? That girl was probably raped and now she's alone in the woods, and these two seem happy about it.'

'No one's happy about it,' shouted Guy. 'But what do you want us to do? The phones are dead. The car's buggered. And the girl has just run off, and in Tracy's clothes too.'

Ash sighed, knowing this argument was getting them nowhere. 'It would just be nice to hear some compassion, that's all.'

'All right guys, enough,' said Nick firmly, fixing them each in turn with his lawyer's gaze. 'Here's the plan of action. We make sure the place is secure, and then wait here the night. That means locking all the windows and doors so there's no way we get any uninvited guests. Then as soon as it's light, we walk down to the main road, or somewhere we can get reception, and call for help. We'll also report what happened to the girl. It'll probably mean the end of the trip, but I think we're all happy to accept that.'

Everyone nodded.

'We've got food, we've got booze, so let's just sit tight.'

'Sounds like a plan,' said Guy, beginning to calm down. 'I need a leak. While I'm up there, I'll lock the windows.'

'Thanks, Guy,' said Nick, patting his friend's shoulder as he walked by. Guy avoided looking at him. It was clear to Ash that what friendship there was between them had just taken a very big hit, and at least part of that was her fault. She smiled at her husband to show she supported what he'd done. He gave her a nod in return before turning away, saying, 'I'll check the back door's locked.'

Tracy sat down heavily on the sofa. 'Jesus, what a day.'

'Tell me about it,' said Ash. She still couldn't get the poor little blonde girl out of her mind. She was so young and so vulnerable. But Nick's words made sense. Right now there was nothing else they could do to help her.

Ash went over to the front window and pulled back the curtain to check that the window was locked. As she did so she was unable to resist looking out into the night. The Land Rover sat sadly in the driveway, and once again Ash wondered who'd tampered with it, and why they'd gone to so much trouble to find the girl.

Something moved at the edge of the treeline. It looked like a person. Ash squinted, pushing her face against the glass, but the figure was gone.

'Is everything all right out there?' asked Tracy uncertainly.

Ash replaced the curtain, trying to decide whether or not to tell Tracy what she'd just seen. Or thought she'd seen anyway. She decided not to. Tracy had had enough scares for one day, and there was no point setting her off again. 'It's fine. Dark, that's all.'

'I'm glad we're in here.'

'So am I,' said Ash, but her heart was beating faster, and she could feel the slow, cold fingers of fear beginning to creep up her spine. If someone was out there watching them, what were they planning on doing?

Tracy stood up. 'I need a glass of wine. Do you want one?'

Ash was checking the lock on

the other window. She saw nothing else outside, and walked back over. 'Sounds good to me,' she said as casually as possible.

'Listen, I'm sorry, Ash. This whole thing's been a bit of a shock, that's all.'

Ash smiled, appreciating the other woman's efforts to make up. 'Yeah, I know. I'm sorry too.'

Tracy gave a small nod and disappeared into the kitchen, returning a minute later with two big glasses of white wine, followed by Nick, who was holding a bottle of Becks. 'It's all locked up at the back,' he said, looking more relaxed. 'We should be safe and sound now.'

'Thank God for that,' said Tracy, clicking glasses with Ash and taking a huge gulp of her wine.

Nick put an arm round Ash's waist, pulling her close. 'You're OK, aren't you, babe?'

She smiled. 'Course I am. I'm tougher than you think.'

'You're tougher than all of us.' He kissed her forehead, and in that moment she realised how much she loved him. Nine years together, and he was still the centre of her universe. That was some achievement.

'What's Guy doing?' said Tracy, her glass already less than half full. She went over to the bottom of the stairs and looked up. 'Guy, what the hell are you doing up there?' she bellowed.

There was no answer.

'Guy?' she called again, louder this time. 'What are you doing?'

But again her words were met only with silence.

CHAPTER FIVE

Suddenly the room felt small, the air heavy.

Tracy's face fell. 'He's not the

sort to play practical jokes,' she said fearfully. 'Is he, Nick?'

Nick shook his head, joining her at the bottom of the staircase. 'Guy, it's Nick. If you're up there, come down right now please.' His voice was loud and confident, but Ash had been with him long enough to detect a faint hint of nerves in it.

Silence.

'I'm scared,' said Tracy. 'I think something might have happened to him.'

Ash was scared too. Really scared. This whole thing felt unreal, like stepping into a nightmare. Except it wasn't a nightmare. It was actually happening, right now. She turned to Nick. 'I thought I saw someone outside. A few minutes ago.'

'Why didn't you say?'

'I thought it might be my imagination.'

Tracy called up to her husband again, her voice sounding a bit hysterical for the first time. 'What

43

are we going to do?' she asked the other two.

'Stay here,' said Nick, striding past them into the kitchen. He came back out a few moments later holding two large kitchen knives. He handed one to Ash. 'We're going to go up.'

Ash stared at the weapon in her hand. The thought of stabbing someone made her feel sick. 'Are you sure we should be doing this?'

'Yes,' he said firmly. 'We don't know who we're dealing with here, so we've got to cover every angle. I'll go up first. Ash, you follow behind me. Trace, I haven't got a weapon you can use, so you stay here.'

Tracy shook her head. 'No way. He's my husband. I'm coming up too.'

'Well, stay behind me. Both of you.'

Ash and Tracy exchanged looks as they started up the stairs behind Nick. Tracy looked just how Ash felt—terrified.

The upstairs landing was long and narrow with a door at either end, and two more doors running along the middle. All of them were closed. The main light was on but nothing moved.

The silence was immense. Ash could hear her husband's steady breathing.

'Guy,' he said, 'if this is a joke, I promise you, without a word of a lie, I will never, repeat never, speak to you again.' He waited, hoping that his friend would jump out of his hiding place and provide them with the only explanation that could make sense.

But he didn't. Nothing happened.

Nick lifted the knife and, as Ash and Tracy crowded on to the landing behind him, he slowly nudged open one of the doors. It was the bathroom. He switched on the light, but stayed outside. It was empty, and far too small for anyone to hide in. There wasn't even a shower curtain.

Nick breathed an audible sigh of relief, and Ash noticed that the knife was shaking in his hand. She also noticed that she was gripping her own weapon so tightly that her knuckles had turned white.

Moving along the landing, Nick nudged open the next door, which Ash knew was the spare bedroom. Again staying outside, he switched on the light.

'He's probably in our bedroom,' said Tracy as they looked inside the empty room, with its untouched bed. 'Maybe he's just gone to sleep.'

'Maybe,' said Nick.

'Maybe we're just being stupid,' continued Tracy with a laugh so false it hurt to hear it. Her voice was cracking. 'We're going to giggle about this in the morning.'

'What's that on the bed covers?' Ash pointed to a couple of spots of red on the far side of the bed that stood out on the white duvet cover.

A faint gurgling sound came from

somewhere in the room, out of sight. Almost a choke but not quite. A human sound.

No one moved. No one said a word. Because they all knew that it came from Guy.

The knife flew out from behind the door, like a snake striking, attached to a gloved hand. It buried itself in Nick's gut.

Tracy screamed. Ash simply watched, caught in slow motion as her husband made a sound like a hiccup, his eyes widening.

The knife was suddenly withdrawn and a figure in black filled up the doorway. He drove the blade into Nick a second time, then shoved him backwards, like he was some kind of annoying shop dummy, sending him crashing over the banister and down the wooden steps.

For a long, terrible second Ash was frozen to the spot, just like she had been during the mugging. The shocking nature of what was happening was too much to take in. Her husband, the man she'd spent almost a third of her life with, her soulmate, her whole life for God's sake, had just been murdered in front of her. He was gone. Just like that.

And she was next.

The killer was big and powerful-looking, with a black hood covering his features. And he was fast. Very fast. He swung round to face her, ready to deal her a blow with the bloodied knife.

It was at this point that Ash finally realised she had to move fast. In one movement she turned and ran, but careered straight into Tracy, who hadn't yet got out of the way, and who was still screaming.

Ash stumbled, losing her balance, and fell forward, letting go of the knife in the process. Out of the corner of her eye she saw Tracy, who was still on her feet, dash for the stairs. Then Ash was rolling round to face her husband's killer, at the same time scrabbling about for the knife.

A drop of Nick's blood fell from the killer's knife blade, splashing her face with a disgusting warmth as he loomed over her. He grabbed Ash by one wrist and yanked her roughly to her feet.

Operating entirely on instinct, she threw a wild punch, catching him full in the face before he had a chance to drive the knife into her. Ash kept fit. She worked out three times a week and had recently started doing boxercise. She thanked God for all these things now because the punch was a good one. It knocked him into the banister and made him loosen his grip on Ash's wrist.

Pulling free, she turned and ran, following Tracy.

But Tracy had stopped at the top of the stairs and was looking down them with an expression of pure terror. 'There's another one coming!' she screamed. 'He's got in the front door!'

Ash didn't even have time to look, let alone take in the fact that there were possibly two of these psychopaths rather than one, and that the other had come through a door that she knew was locked. She didn't even look back towards her husband, because there was no time for that. Her survival instinct had kicked in. She sprinted the length of the landing, towards the door to the bedroom she and Nick should have been sharing that night, yelling at Tracy to come with her.

Ash hit the door at a run, flinging it open without even giving a thought to who might be behind it. She could hear Tracy right behind her and she hauled her in. As the dark figure of the killer moved towards them she slammed the door shut, noticing with huge relief that there was a key in the lock. Pressing her whole body against the door, she turned it with shaking hands. She could hear him outside, his breathing calm and steady, as he tried and failed to turn the handle.

A split second later the door shook on its hinges as he slammed into it from the other side. It was only a small lock and she knew it wasn't going to hold for more than a few seconds.

They were trapped.

The door shook again, and this time she heard the sound of wood splitting.

Looking round desperately, Ash spotted the sash window. It was the only way out. Vaulting the bed, she dashed over and flicked the catch on the lower window, yanking it upwards as hard as she could. The drop to the patio below was a good fifteen feet, but they had no choice.

'Come on!' she screamed at Tracy, who was still staring at the door. 'Move it!'

Tracy ran over, took one look through the window, and turned to Ash. She started to say something, but Ash wasn't listening. As the door shook once again, almost giving way this time, she grabbed Tracy by the collar and pushed her into the gap. 'Go! Go! Go!' she screamed, clambering out after her.

Tracy jumped, letting out a long shriek, at just the moment when the door flew open and the killer came striding into the room. He made straight for Ash with the bloodied knife raised, like something out of one of those horror films that had always scared her as a teenager.

Ash threw her legs out of the window and slid through it, grabbing at the window ledge with both hands as she swung round, hoping to lessen the distance between herself and the ground before she jumped. But as she let go a gloved hand grabbed her wrist. Suddenly she was dangling helplessly in mid-air. The killer began to lift her back up with an almost unbelievable strength, while bringing his knife hand down in the direction of her throat.

Knowing she had just seconds left, Ash pulled and struggled with all her might, wriggling like a fish on the line, and the next second she was falling through the air.

Ash hit the tarmac feet first and a stinging pain shot up her legs. She rolled over and leaped to her feet. Tracy was already staggering towards the trees a few yards away. Ash caught her up and grabbed her by the arm, dragging her along as she tried to put as much distance between them and the house as possible.

'I'm hurt,' whined Tracy, slowing down. 'I think I've broken my ankle.'

'I don't care!' hissed Ash, staring her right in the eye as they fought their way into the forest. 'Run on it. You've got no choice.'

For a long moment, Ash thought about leaving Tracy behind, knowing she'd be far quicker on her own. But she stopped herself, because she knew she'd never be able to live with the guilt if she bolted now.

She took a quick glance over her shoulder and thought she saw a figure moving just inside the trees. It spurred her into running even faster. This time Tracy kept up, although she was limping badly and her face was taut with pain. What was truly terrifying Ash was the fact that these men, whoever they were, hadn't uttered a single word. They were going about their murderous work as if it was the most natural thing in the world.

Ash had no idea why the four of them were being targeted. It had to be something to do with the girl, but she wasn't even with them now, so why were they still coming? Whatever the reason, Ash had an awful feeling that they weren't going to stop until she and Tracy were dead.

They were tearing through the branches now, ignoring the bushes and brambles that slashed at them, concentrating everything on escape. These were big woods. There would be plenty of places to hide. They could find somewhere, then wait for morning and raise the alarm.

Ash felt the first stirrings of hope. They were moving fast and there were no sounds of pursuit. Tracy was in pain, but adrenalin and fear were driving them both on, deeper and deeper into the forest.

Then her friend let out a terrible scream and Ash's hope vanished.

CHAPTER SIX

Tracy went down hard, rolling over in the dirt. For a split second Ash thought her ankle was in fact broken, but it was worse than that. Much worse.

A mantrap, the type used by hunters, had slammed shut on one of her legs, its metal teeth digging deep into the flesh. Tracy wailed in pain as she sat up and tried to pull it off. Ash immediately crouched down and tried to help. But the damn thing wouldn't budge. It was stuck fast.

'Help me, Ash, please . . .'

'Hush, Trace,' whispered Ash, still pulling on the rusty clamps. 'You've got to be quiet.' But it was hard to keep the panic out of her voice. She knew that even if she did free Tracy, there was no way she was going to be able to run any further. Her leg looked in a bad way. Blood was seeping through her jeans in a dozen places.

Tracy knew it too. Ash could see the terrified hopelessness in her eyes.

'Please don't leave me.'

'I won't,' Ash told her with a determination she didn't feel. 'You've just got to be quiet. They might hear us.'

She stopped what she was doing and listened to the silence, trying to work out how far they'd come from the lodge. She could no longer see its lights, and guessed they'd made a few hundred metres. The leaves here were thick, and there was a large knot of brambles a few feet away, which they could probably hide under without being seen. If she could just move Tracy and keep her quiet.

The mantrap was attached by a thick piece of rusty wire to a bolt sticking barely an inch out of the ground. Ash started to dig the bolt out using her bare hands, figuring it was quicker to move Tracy with the mantrap still attached to her than to keep trying to remove it from her leg.

'Oh God,' whispered Tracy. 'It hurts so much.'

Ash gave her a reassuring smile, truly feeling for her then. 'It's going to be OK, I promise.'

As she lifted her head and listened again to the quietness of the forest, trying to pick up any sound of pursuit, she heard it.

The baying of dogs.

And it was coming closer.

Tracy and Ash exchanged glances. Tears began to stream down Tracy's face now as the realisation that this was the end of the line took hold. 'Oh God no. Please, Ash. Please don't leave me. I don't want to die.' Her voice was rising, affected by the same panic that was also rising up in Ash like an unstoppable force, making her whole body shake, as if it was about to go into spasm.

'I won't,' hissed Ash, redoubling her efforts to dig out the bolt, even though she knew it wouldn't do any good. 'I swear it. I won't.'

The dogs, and there were at least two of them, were getting closer. Ash could hear their progress up the hill. She knew that they'd be on them at any moment. Ash had to make a decision. Did she stay here with Tracy and suffer the consequences, or did she try to save herself?

She looked at Tracy.

Tracy looked back, her face crumpled in the moonlight, because she knew what Ash was going to do. What she had no choice but to do.

Ash had always told herself that she wouldn't be able to live without Nick. That if anything happened to him she'd want to die too, because life without him would be meaningless. But when it came down to it, that was bullshit. She wanted to live. To see the world. To watch the sun set. To smell the flowers. To make the most of everything out there that she'd previously taken for granted.

'I'm sorry,' she whispered, and jumped to her feet. 'Please forgive me.'

Tracy let out a howl of terror so intense and painful that for a moment it even silenced the dogs. Ash couldn't bear to look at her. She knew that she was sentencing an innocent woman to death. But what else could she do?

Ash took off at a sprint, keeping hold of her emotions, focusing her mind and watching the ground closely for any sign of another trap. There'd be a time for mourning, and for guilt, later. Right now she had to do what it took to survive. She was hugely thankful that she'd invested so much time and effort in keeping herself in shape. There was no way she'd be able to outrun dogs, but they'd be delayed for a short time at least with Tracy, and there were ways and means of putting them off her scent. As she ran, she pulled off the fleece she'd been wearing all day. She kept it down by her side, looking out for a good place to drop it.

A scream pierced the cool night air, shrill and terrible as it echoed through the trees.

And then it abruptly stopped. Cut off in mid-stride.

Ash knew that it meant Tracy was dead, and that they'd be after her now.

She dropped the fleece and changed direction.

CHAPTER SEVEN

They killed the girl quickly. Stuart picked her up from behind, held her steady, and then cut her throat in one swift movement, while Rory held the dogs and watched, shaking his head.

'This is a big problem,' he said. 'We're going to get a lot of shit for this. Eastern European whores are ten a penny, they don't get missed. But these are tourists. The boss is going to be mighty pissed off.'

'We've just got to make sure they disappear,' said Stuart, stepping away from the girl as she twitched on the ground. The mantrap round her leg made a scratching sound against the soil.

That, thought Rory, was the problem with his younger brother. He didn't realise that you couldn't just kill your way out of trouble. You had to plan it. 'You fucked up, Stuart. Don't ever do that again.'

'I won't. The little bitch tricked me, but it was a one-off.'

Rory gave a curt nod. 'It better be.'

In the five years they'd been guarding the whores who were delivered to the estate, they'd never once had a problem. The girls tended to be young and they were usually too scared and confused even to think of escape, which was just the way it should be. Rory prided himself on his ability to run things smoothly, but they'd grown far too complacent lately. He hadn't even been there today when the girl got out. Then Stuart had totally messed up by delaying it a good ten minutes before he called him, which had given her the chance to cover some distance. Just their luck, she ran into what must have been the only bunch of tourists for twenty miles.

The tourists had to die in order to protect the secret. Rory had to make sure it didn't get out into the wider world. If anyone else had made that kind of mistake, Rory wouldn't have hesitated to put him in the ground with all the other bodies from the last five years. But Stuart was family, and you didn't do that to family.

On the ground, the girl stopped twitching. Stuart gave her a kick just to check that she was dead, although with half her head hanging off she was always going to be.

Rory let out a deep breath, and looked into the wall of trees ahead. 'Three down, one to go. Let's find her and then we can go home for the night.'

He released the dogs, watching as they tore off into the darkness. Then he pulled out his knife, stepped over the girl's corpse, and headed after them.

CHAPTER EIGHT

Only when her lungs felt close to bursting did Ash finally slow down to a walk.

It felt like she'd come a long way but she'd seen no break in the forest. It seemed to be going on for ever. Behind her, in the distance, she could still hear the dogs barking, but it sounded like they'd stopped. She guessed that they'd found her fleece. Since then she'd yanked off her bra from beneath her T-shirt and hung that from a branch, before changing direction again. She was doing everything she could think of to put the dogs off her trail.

But she couldn't keep removing items of clothing. She didn't have enough of them. And as soon as she stopped doing it, the dogs would be on her. Ash was going to have to come up with a different plan because the people hunting her were clearly determined.

The naked girl who'd run into them earlier was obviously connected to some kind of criminal activity. She was possibly even a criminal herself. Ash now regretted the fact that they'd stopped to help her. If they'd just sent her on her way and kept walking, like it was nothing to do with them (which it hadn't been), none of this would have happened. They could have been sitting round a warm fire, enjoying a glass of wine and the cold meat and salad supper Ash had brought up with her from London. Guy could have wittered on about what a fantastic place Singapore was to do business in. Tracy could have bored them all talking about her massages and her tennis and her cocktail hours on the balcony of some sun-drenched hotel. And she and Nick could have exchanged knowing glances and dreamed of ripping each other's clothes off as soon as they hit the bedroom.

Oh God, Nick.

It was all gone. Everything. The most shocking thing was how quickly it had all happened. It couldn't have been more much than an hour since they'd been walking along the ridge towards home, with just the wild scenery for company. Now the lives of the three people she'd shared the day with were over. The man she'd been married to for seven years had been snatched away from her in the blink of an eye by another man he'd never met before, and never done a thing to. There hadn't even been a chance for her to hold him in her arms and say goodbye.

Ash felt the tears sting her cheeks. That murdering bastard. If only he knew what he'd done. But he didn't. He didn't know and he didn't care. And it was certain that he, and whoever else he was with, wanted to do exactly the same thing to her too.

The barking was getting closer again, and by the sound of it the dogs were moving fast. They'd probably be heading for the abandoned bra, but Ash couldn't rely on that fact. She needed to keep moving and hope that she came across a house, or farm, or anywhere she could summon help. It wasn't much of a plan, but the alternative was climbing a tree, and that wasn't going to work either.

Still panting from all the running she'd done already, she set off again, picking up speed, trying to work out whether she should get rid of her T-shirt next, or one of her socks.

The barking was still coming towards her, and it was getting closer.

She accelerated, going as fast as she could. The forest was beginning to open out now with more space between the trees and fewer bushes to hide behind. The treetops had thinned out too, making it lighter and easier for Ash to be spotted. She looked up, silently cursing the moon, then looked back down, watching out for traps.

One of the dogs howled, no more than fifty metres behind her. Fifty metres and closing.

Ash was flying now. She didn't think she'd ever run this fast, not even when she was a thirteen-year-old girl and the champion sprinter in her year at school, capable of doing a hundred metres in just over twelve and a half seconds. Her long, gangly legs used to 'eat up the track like spaghetti', as her mum would say. But that didn't matter now because she was never going to be able to go fast enough. The dogs were going to catch her. In a few minutes' time it was all going to be over. Every experience she had ever had, every emotion she'd ever felt, was going to disappear for ever, wiped clean. It would be like she'd never existed.

The hole appeared without

warning, and her foot went straight into it. She tripped and landed painfully on the hard ground.

Suddenly she was rolling down an incline, hitting stones and exposed tree roots before landing with an icy splash in water.

She was in a fast-moving stream about ten metres across. Rolling further into it, she allowed herself to be taken by the current, keeping all but the top half of her head underwater as she half-crawled and half-swam downstream. The water was freezing but she didn't care. This was her chance of escape.

Behind her, Ash heard the dogs stop, barking wildly. She dipped her head below the surface, holding her breath, pushing herself into the middle where the water was three or four feet deep and she could swim properly. A minute passed and she came up, gasping for air.

The stream was running faster now, and she could hear a roaring, growing steadily louder, coming from further ahead. That was when she realised with a jolt of panic that she'd read in a brochure at the lodge that close by was a waterfall more than twenty metres high.

She must be heading straight for it.

Cursing, she fought her way across to the opposite side of the stream from the dogs, but she was soon out of her depth, and fully clothed and wearing shoes. It was suddenly a terrible struggle. The roar was getting louder, and she was being swept along faster. Currents of water were whirling and flowing around her, and the cold was beginning to have a real effect.

For a moment she thought about giving up. Just letting the water take her to where it would. If that meant death, then so be it. At least that way the effort was over.

But Ash was a fighter. She always had been. When she put her mind to something she didn't give up.

An exposed rock appeared in front of her, and she grabbed hold of it. She took a couple of desperate, panting breaths before using the rock as a lever to push herself over to another rock closer to the bank. A huge sense of relief filled her as she felt solid ground beneath her feet. She waded out, glancing backwards. She could still hear the dogs but they sounded quite a long way back now, and because they were on the other side of the stream, she hoped they'd no longer have her scent.

Close to exhaustion now, and shivering with the cold, Ash crawled under a thick holly bush a few yards from the water's edge, trying to get as far under it as possible. Finally, she lay still and let her breathing slow.

In those moments, she once again thought about death, about how a person's world could change in the blink of an eye, or the deep slash of a knife. One minute she was a happily married woman living a problem-free life. The next her husband was lying dead in their holiday home, and she was alone and terrified in the woods while at least one killer hunted her down for a reason she simply couldn't understand. Why could they possibly want to kill her? She didn't even have any idea who they were.

Ash lay there for what felt like a long time. A minute? Two? Five? It was difficult to tell, and she didn't dare look at her watch. However long it was, she heard no further sound from her pursuers or the dogs. Had they given up and gone? Or were they still out there waiting for her to make her move? God, she was so very, very cold. She couldn't lie like this for ever. At some point she would have to find shelter. Otherwise she risked dying from exposure.

A twig snapped a few yards away, and Ash froze.

CHAPTER NINE

Silence followed. One second. Two seconds. Three. Ash stopped breathing and fought to keep her shivering under control, because it was rustling the leaves under her. Every nerve ending in her body felt like it was on fire.

She heard a footstep nearby. Then another. Coming closer.

Oh God, no.

She didn't want to die. The thought of a knife being plunged into her and slowly bleeding to death almost made her cry out in utter terror. But she forced herself to calm down, hold her breath and stay still. Without the dogs to help him there was a possibility he might miss her. No part of her body was exposed. He might not see her.

Please God, if you exist, help me now. Don't let him see me. Please.

The man was right above her now. She could feel his presence. His boots crunched on the forest floor as he crept round the bush.

Don't move. Don't speak. Don't breathe.

Slowly Ash forced her eyes open, and that was when she saw the bottom half of his legs. He was standing right there, his muddied boots only two feet from her head, pointing her way.

Jesus, he knows I'm here.

The whole thing felt like some horrible game of hide and seek. Ash could feel her lungs coming close to bursting. She had to breathe soon.

Then he was moving off again, down towards the edge of the stream. As he did so, more of him came into view. It was the same man from the lodge. The one who'd stabbed Nick. She was sure of it. He was still holding the bloodied knife he'd used down by his side.

Bastard.

Out of the corner of her eye, Ash could see a piece of jagged flint the size of a fist near to her right hand. Suddenly she felt an intense rage the like of which she'd never experienced before. Ash considered herself a nice girl who didn't believe in the death penalty, but at that moment all she wanted to do was kill this bastard who'd come here and ruined her life. She allowed herself a long, silent breath before reaching out for the piece of flint and gripping it tightly.

The man in black crouched down and looked up and down the stream.

Then slowly he began to turn, and Ash realised that at the height he was at, he was going to see her.

Fear rushed back. It mixed with rage and desperation. All these different emotions tore around her body like the whirlpools in the stream. She had to make a decision. Fast.

He turned round completely. He was wearing night vision goggles and he was staring straight at her.

For a split second, he didn't move.

But Ash did.

With a speed born of pure heart-pounding adrenalin, she leaped out of the bush, rose to her full height and let out a howl of anger as she threw the stone straight at his head.

It was her one chance of survival, and it worked. The stone hit him full in the face, knocking him backwards.

He kept his balance, and he still had the knife, but he was hurt. He clutched at his face with his free hand and grunted with pain.

Now that she'd drawn blood, the rage seemed to re-energise Ash. She flew forward, picked up the stone and, before her attacker had time to defend himself, smashed it into the side of his head with such force that he went down to his knees.

He swung his knife at her in a wild arc but he was way too slow and unsteady. Ash dodged out of the way and danced round the back of him, sensing victory as she struck him in the base of the skull with another big howl.

This time the knife dropped from his hand and he let out a painful groan as he fell forward.

Ash was on him like a shot, jumping on his back and forcing him into the dirt. She brought the stone down again and again on his head, using both hands for effect, ignoring the terrible sound of bone crunching and the blood and brain matter oozing out of his skull. She was lost in the absolute thrill of revenge.

Then, without warning, it was like a switch had been turned off. Ash stopped hitting him, let the stone fall from her hands, and began to sob. He'd stopped moving, and the top of his head was a white-flecked pulp of meat and shattered bone. The man who'd killed her husband was dead, and Ash was the one who'd killed him.

Filled with a black curiosity,

needing to know what a murderer like him looked like, she reached down with a shaking hand and pulled off the goggles.

He was younger than her, probably no more than late twenties with pale, unlined features and plump cheeks with a heavy spray of freckles. His eyes were closed, and it looked like he was asleep. And that was the thing. He looked so bloody normal. There was no menace about him, no sign of the darkness that must have been in his heart. As she stared, a thick line of blood ran down his forehead and pooled in his eye.

'Oh God,' whispered Ash. 'What have I done?'

Which was the moment when she heard an angry bark. She looked up and saw a second black-clad figure on the other side of the stream, running down towards her and pulling a rifle from his shoulder. The dogs, sleek-looking Dobermanns, were on either side of him.

'Get her, boys!' he roared.

The baying dogs charged into the stream while the man went down on one knee, taking a firing stance.

Calling up her last reserves of energy, Ash turned and bolted, hurtling through bushes, keeping low, trying to zigzag so she wouldn't present him with a decent target. She knew she'd never outrun the dogs, but she had no choice but to try.

A shot rang out with a loud crack, and a bullet whistled through the branches so close to Ash that she could almost feel its heat.

Her legs ached. Her whole body felt like it was seizing up. Fit or not, there was no way she could last much longer.

Keep going. Your life depends on it. If you stop, you die.

A branch hit her in the face, cutting the skin just beneath her eye. She almost fell but somehow righted herself, hearing the dogs getting closer once again.

Then suddenly the ground disappeared in front of her and Ash was forced to make an emergency stop. She only just avoided falling over the edge of a high cliff that dropped down to a river flowing hard a long, long way below. Thirty metres to her left, the waterfall cascaded down to meet it. The water sparkled in the moonlight that flickered through the trees.

Ash turned as the dogs came bolting out of the trees straight at her, teeth bared, tongues lolling. She'd always been petrified of heights. She refused to travel in cable cars, and didn't even like going up a stepladder at home. But people can overcome even their worst fears when confronted by two attack dogs, and the prospect of certain death.

As the first dog leaped for her she turned and jumped out into the unknown, eyes squeezed shut and legs flapping wildly. She was half-expecting the sensation of teeth sinking into her flesh, but nothing came. Instead she simply fell through space for what seemed like hours, her whole life flashing before her— visions of childhood parties, desert islands, romantic nights with Nick.

She hit the water with a huge crash, and felt herself being taken further and further downstream. Ash fought all the time to keep her head above water and avoid the warm embrace of unconsciousness.

The last thing she remembered was the current driving her into the shallows where she could feel the ground beneath her feet.

Then, finally, everything went black.

CHAPTER TEN

Slowly, ever so slowly, Ash's eyes opened.

For a few seconds she had no idea

where she was, just this vague feeling that she'd had a dark and brutal dream in which her beloved Nick had been murdered. Then, as she raised her head from where it had been face down in foul-smelling mud, and felt her whole body aching, she remembered what had happened, and her heart sank.

Rubbing mud from her eyes, she carefully glanced round. Sunlight dappled through the trees, and she was forced to squint against it. By the sun's low angle she guessed it was fairly early in the morning.

She rolled round on to her back with a groan and saw that water was lapping at her hiking shoes. She was lying next to a fast-flowing river, with a cliff stretching up on the other side. The river must have carried her along for God knows how far before depositing her here in a flat clearing.

As she slowly sat up, Ash felt a rush of sickness that immediately set off a bout of shivering. She was in a bad way. But at least she was alive. Somehow, against all the odds, she'd made it. And somehow they hadn't found her, even though she must have been unconscious for hours.

Ash got to her feet, cold and sick but determined not to break down and cry over what had happened to Nick. Which was when she remembered that she'd killed one of them herself. *Killed him.* It was hard to accept that she, Ash, a primary school teacher by trade who hadn't had a fight since she was thirteen years old (with Chloe Baxter about a boy in the dinner queue), had beaten a man so badly that his brains had come out. Jesus. It made her want to throw up.

Pulling a thick knot of matted hair out of her eyes, she staggered through the trees. How on earth was she ever going to explain what had happened the previous night to anyone? She still wasn't sure why she, Nick and the others had been targeted. But at least now that it was daytime, she felt less scared. There was something about the sunshine that lifted her spirits.

The woods were empty and filled with the sound of birdsong. It was a real contrast to the previous night. No baying of hounds, or screams of dying friends. She thought about Tracy then. Poor, frightened Tracy caught in a metal trap and left to die alone.

'It wasn't your fault,' Ash told herself. 'You did what you had to do.'

Even so, it didn't make her feel any better.

The forest began to thin out, and the sunshine became brighter ahead. Ash sped up, telling herself that soon she'd be able to rest, that it wouldn't be much longer before she found someone. Just one more big effort and this would all be over.

Suddenly the trees parted in front of her and she was standing on a narrow pot-holed road. On the other side was an overgrown field that stretched up towards another pine-covered hill.

She looked down, never so pleased to see tarmac in her life. It was a sign, however minor, of life—something she felt she'd left behind. It filled her with a renewed sense of hope.

She looked left and saw a stone cottage on the corner thirty metres away. Smoke rose from its chimney, and a battered old Land Rover sat on its dirt driveway.

A new emotion mixed with the hope, one she'd become used to in the last twelve hours. Fear. This could be where the men hunting her lived. They had to live somewhere, and it was likely to be close by. Had the girl, the one who'd caused them so much trouble, escaped from here? If she had, it would explain why they'd been so keen to silence Ash and the others, to prevent them from reporting what they'd seen to the police and leading them back here.

She took a deep breath, trying to work out what to do. The problem was she had no idea where she was. She reached into her jeans pocket and pulled out her mobile, hoping for a reception, but it wouldn't even turn on. The water had ruined it.

Standing in the road shivering, Ash felt utterly drained of energy. It could be miles to the next house, and she wasn't at all sure how much longer she could keep going. She was sick. She was being hunted down. She needed help.

The front door to the cottage opened. Ash instinctively jumped out of sight behind a tree.

A well-built older lady with her silver hair in a bun stepped outside. She had a basket in her hands and was wearing a navy dress and an old-fashioned white pinafore. Even from a distance, Ash could see she had a kindly, round face.

But Ash had had her world torn apart these past few hours and the experience had made her very careful. The old lady hadn't seen her so Ash waited and watched as she walked round the side of the cottage and passed out of sight, singing softly to herself as she went.

Keeping inside the treeline, Ash crept towards the cottage, stopping when she saw the old lady bent over, feeding half a dozen chickens in a coop. She was cooing at them in a lilting Scottish accent as she threw the feed, looking as if she hadn't a care in the world. The sight of her made Ash's eyes fill with tears.

Slowly, awkwardly, she stepped out from the trees. 'Excuse me . . .'

The old lady jumped, then turned her way, putting a hand to her mouth, her bright blue eyes widening. 'Gosh, my love. You scared me.'

'I'm sorry.' Ash took another unsteady step forward, trying to stop herself from breaking down. 'I've been hurt.' The tears were streaming down her face now.

The old lady opened her two beefy arms and Ash fell into them, sobbing into her shoulder, breathing in comforting smells of lavender and baking.

'There there, my love,' the old lady whispered into her ear, her grip surprisingly strong. 'You're going to catch a death of cold out here. Let's get you inside, into the warm.'

The old lady put down her basket, ignoring the frantic clucking of the chickens, and led Ash into the cottage through a side door. Ash found herself in a surprisingly spacious, if tired-looking, kitchen.

'You sit down there, young lady,' she said, pointing at a wooden table with stools in one corner, 'and I'll get you a blanket.'

Ash leaned back against the stone wall, wrapping her arms round herself in an effort to stay warm.

The kitchen was cluttered with pots and pans, cooking utensils and dog-eared recipe books, and there was a faint damp smell that was mixed with the smell of fresh bread. A tray containing a newly baked loaf sat on the ancient cooker. On the opposite wall, an equally old picture of the Cheshire Cat from *Alice in Wonderland* grinned at her. Ash even managed a small grin in return. For the first time since this nightmare had begun, she found herself able to relax.

'What happened to you, my love?' asked the old lady, returning with a thick spotted blanket.

Ash saw no reason not to tell her the truth. Wrapping herself in the blanket, she gave her a brief description of the previous night's events, starting from when they'd run into the girl. She kept the drama down to a minimum but told her that her husband and two friends had been killed.

The old lady looked shocked, which was no great surprise, and put a hand to her mouth. 'And this all happened round here, you say? Here in these woods?'

Ash nodded numbly. 'Yes.'

'I've lived here all my life, my love, and I've never heard of anything like this. I don't understand where this naked girl could have come from. There's nothing here but national park and the shooting estate over near Wood End, but that's owned by one of those banker types in London you never see. It all seems very strange. Men chasing this girl, then chasing you and your friends, trying to kill you. Whatever happened to the girl?'

'I don't know.'

The old lady was right. The whole thing was strange, like something out of a cheap horror film. For a moment, Ash wondered if she actually was going mad. But then she pulled herself together. It *had* happened. All of it. Just as she remembered.

'I'm not lying, Mrs . . .'

'Dora. Call me Dora.' She smiled. 'I'm not saying you are, my love. I can see you've had a terrible time of it.'

'I need to call the police. My phone's broken. Do you have a phone here?'

'Course I do,' said Dora with a laugh. 'We might live out in the sticks, but we're not in the nineteenth century.'

'I'm sorry, I didn't mean it like that,' said Ash, wrapping herself even tighter in the blanket.

Dora put a reassuring hand on her shoulder. 'I know you didn't, my love. Now you wait here while I call the police. Then I'll come back and make you something to eat.'

Ash nodded. 'Thank you.'

Dora left the room for a second time and Ash got to her feet, the effort making her wince. She could tell the old lady didn't believe her story, but she wasn't surprised. It was not an easy one to believe. Three murders, possibly four, as well as at least two killers, all in the same quiet forest in the middle of nowhere. Ash wouldn't have believed it either. She'd think the person telling the story was high on some particularly intense drugs. But in the end it didn't matter as long as she called the police. Then they could deal with it.

She could hear Dora's voice in the next room talking on the phone and she walked slowly over to the door. As Ash stepped into the living room, Dora put the phone down and turned round. 'They're on their way, my love, but they won't be here for a good twenty minutes. We're a long way from the station here.' She wiped her hands on her pinafore. 'Let me make you some hot breakfast.'

The thought of food made Ash feel sick. 'It's all right, Dora,' she said with a weak smile, 'I'm really not hungry.'

'But you must eat something.'

'Please, can I just have a cup of tea?'

Dora tried not to look disappointed. 'As you wish, my love. I'll get the kettle on.'

'Do you have a toilet I could use?'

'We certainly do, my love. It's even an inside one.' She winked and grinned playfully at Ash as she pointed to a door beside the staircase.

'I really appreciate this,' Ash told her. She thought about asking for a shower too but decided against it since she'd only have to get back into her wet clothes afterwards.

'It's the least I can do,' said Dora, shuffling past her into the kitchen.

Something was wrong. Ash had no idea what it was but it was worrying her. Was Dora hiding something? Or was Ash just imagining it? Had the events of the previous night made her so paranoid that she was now suspicious of everything, including even a friendly old lady?

A friendly old lady who lived out in the woods near to where a mass murder had been committed, but who seemed unconcerned by what had happened.

Ash locked the toilet door behind her and took a deep breath, telling herself to calm down. A mirror in dire need of a clean hung on the bare wall just above the sink. Ash wanted to weep when she saw herself in it. She looked exactly like she felt. Her face was puffy and bruised beneath smears of encrusted dirt, and there were scratches all across her cheeks and forehead. One eye was swollen and black, and her thick auburn hair, usually one of her best features, looked like it belonged on a scarecrow. But it was the haunted expression in her eyes that affected her the most. For a good ten seconds she stared at her reflection, finding it difficult to accept it.

Yet when she'd suddenly stepped out of nowhere in Dora's garden, rather than run a mile the old lady had been kind enough to take her in. Ash was suddenly ashamed for suspecting Dora of meaning her harm.

That was until she turned and saw something on the floor, poking out from just behind the toilet, and her hand went to her mouth to stifle the gasp.

CHAPTER ELEVEN

Ash bent down, carefully picked up the heavily bloodstained ball of tissue, and touched it. The blood was dry, but from its colour she could tell it wasn't very old.

She slipped the tissue back behind the toilet, and her hand brushed against something else. It felt like a picture frame. She pulled it out and stared at the faded photograph behind the glass.

It had been taken outside the front of the cottage. Dora was standing in the centre, wearing a bright floral dress and a big smile. She looked a good ten years younger. Flanking her were two unsmiling teenage boys with pale faces and red hair, one three or four years older than the other. It was obvious from their red hair and freckled faces that they were brothers.

It was also obvious that the younger of the two was the man she'd killed the previous night.

Ash swallowed, squinting at the photo. It might have been taken a long time back, and Ash might have been sick and exhausted, but she was absolutely sure it was him. It wasn't the kind of face she was ever going to forget.

She put the photo back where she'd found it and stood up, no longer able to think about going to the toilet. She had to get out of there. The man she'd killed was Dora's son and she'd bet her life that the second man hunting them, the one who'd shot at her in the woods, was the other son. Did they live here? It would explain the bloody tissue. It might also explain the fact that the photo was shoved behind the toilet rather than hanging on the wall where it could be seen. The other son would have known that Ash had seen his brother's face, so would want any evidence of his identity hidden just in case she, Ash, showed up.

Which almost certainly meant that Dora was a part of this too.

But why would an elderly woman be involved in murder, not to mention the possible kidnapping and rape of young foreign women? That's what Ash simply couldn't understand.

It didn't matter. What mattered

was that she got out of there, and fast.

After flushing the toilet, she slowly opened the door and stepped out into the hallway. She could hear Dora singing to herself in soft, lilting tones in the kitchen. It set Ash's teeth on edge, because the sound seemed so wrong coming from a woman who'd given birth to the two psychopaths who'd hunted her and her friends down. She looked over at the phone in the corner of the living room, wondering who it was Dora had been phoning. She was sure now that it hadn't been the police.

Heart hammering in her chest, Ash crept over and picked up the phone, glancing over her shoulder to check that Dora was still busy before pressing the redial button.

The call went straight to a recorded message for a mobile phone.

Not the police.

Ash took a deep breath, put down

the phone, and started towards the front door. As soon as she was outside she'd make a break for it, head back into the forest, try to find another house somewhere. There had to be someone round here who wasn't involved in whatever the hell was going on.

She tried to turn the handle but it didn't move. The door was locked and there was no sign of a key.

'What's wrong, my love? Where are you going? I've got your tea here.'

Ash turned round far too quickly, like a naughty schoolkid who's been caught doing something wrong. She tried to look as casual as possible. 'I was just going outside for some fresh air. I don't feel too good.'

'Sorry, I always keep that door double-locked.'

No, you don't. I saw you walk out of it ten minutes ago.

'Why don't you sit down and have a nice cup of tea?' Dora smiled and held up the steaming mug. 'The police'll be here soon.'

'If I could just go outside.'

'Of course you can, my love. No one's stopping you. Go out through the kitchen door. Take your tea with you.' She stepped aside, still smiling.

Ash could feel the adrenalin coursing through her, yet the situation seemed so utterly unreal that she was actually worried about appearing rude. 'Thanks,' she said. 'I just need a few gulps of fresh air.'

'Course you do, my love. You've had a hard time of it.'

Dora held out the mug and Ash took it, instinctively putting it to her lips.

The old lady watched her carefully. She had incredibly bright blue eyes. There was a warmth in them that seemed to drag Ash right in. 'Drink, my love,' she said quietly.

Ash felt dizzy and exhausted. She so wanted to sip the tea, to feel its warmth running through her. To sit down and forget all the terrible things that had happened.

Something glinted in Dora's eyes, something cold and triumphant, and the spell was broken.

'I'll have it in a minute.' Ash smiled and turned to put the mug down, every nerve and muscle in her body ready for flight.

With remarkable speed, Dora's hand flew out, knocking the boiling hot tea all over Ash's face and upper body.

Ash screamed in shock and pain and leaped backwards. Dora grabbed her wrist and yanked her back, then placed her in a fierce headlock that immediately choked off Ash's air supply.

The old lady's grip was incredibly strong. Ash's vision began to blur as she fought to break free, trying but failing to dig her elbow into Dora's ribs. What little strength she had left was fading fast. Her whole body soon felt like it was on fire.

'You little whore,' hissed Dora in her ear. 'You murdered my son. You're going to pay for that. We're going to have you begging for your life.'

Ash tried to shout out to her, to ask why, what had she ever done to deserve this? All she wanted to do was go home to her family. But all that came out was a long, drawn-out rasping sound. Blue lights flickered in front of Ash's eyes. She was passing out. She wasn't going to make it.

She had to. There was no choice.

Ash Murray does not give up.

With one last burst of energy, she brought her heel down hard on Dora's toes. The old lady yelped, her grip loosened, and Ash yanked herself out of it. She swung round and punched Dora hard in the face, finding it hard to accept the fact that now she was violently assaulting a senior citizen.

Dora cried out and tumbled back

on to her threadbare sofa, one hand on her jaw, a shocked expression on her face. It looked as if she couldn't believe Ash would do such a horrible thing as punch an old woman. 'You slut!' she screamed, her features screwing up into a mask of fury. 'I'll have you for that!'

But Ash was already out of the room and running through the kitchen, pulling open the door, knowing the woods and freedom were only yards away . . .

She stopped dead. He was in the doorway, a huge man dressed all in black, a mask covering his face. Looking just like the man who'd murdered Nick, even down to the knife he carried in one gloved hand.

'Oh God.'

The fight went out of Ash then. It was replaced by a dark and heavy acceptance that the end had come.

She tried to run back the way she'd come, but he was on her in a second, wrapping his arms round her in a massive bearhug and lifting her up. The tip of the knife blade sat painfully against her throat as he walked her further into the kitchen, her legs flailing uselessly beneath her.

'Ah, I see you've met my other son,' said Dora. The smile was gone from her face, replaced by a dirty scowl. 'Now don't fuck things up this time, Rory. Keep hold of her. She's a feisty little whore.'

'She's nae going anywhere, Ma,' grunted Rory. 'Not this time.'

Ash screamed, the effort making her lungs ache. Her throat hurt where it pushed into the blade, cutting the skin.

Dora, the big jolly lady in dress and pinafore, just laughed and opened up one of the kitchen cupboards. She removed a bottle of dark liquid and a filthy-looking rag. She poured a generous slug of the liquid on to the rag, keeping her face turned away from it. 'Scream all you like, my love,' she said, coming closer. 'Only the animals will hear you out here.'

'Please,' gasped Ash, making one last effort to save herself. 'I just want to go home.'

Dora shook her head, almost sadly. 'Sorry, my love, but that's not going to happen.'

She lifted her hand and pushed the rag into Ash's face. The whole of Ash's world seemed to explode.

CHAPTER TWELVE

Ash Murray dreamed strange dreams. Sometimes she saw her mother's face in them, smiling down at her. Then her mother's face would turn into Dora's, and Dora would be forcing medicine into Ash's mouth, holding her nose to make her drink it, singing nursery rhymes as she worked, the rhymes taking Ash back to the sunny white days of her childhood . . .

Her eyes snapped open and everything seemed terribly bright. She blinked rapidly, turning her head from side to side. Something tight and itchy had been placed round her neck. She looked up and saw the rope tied round a crossbeam a few feet above her head. That was when Ash realised that she was wearing a noose. Her head felt thick and heavy, as if she had a really bad hangover. Her mouth was so dry she couldn't even swallow.

Looking round, she saw that she was back in the living room in the lodge. Daylight flowed in through the windows, and she could hear birdsong coming from outside. She gasped when she saw Nick's body lying sprawled at the foot of the staircase, one leg twisted at a weird angle, where it had caught under a step. Thankfully his face was turned away from her. He was wearing the same clothes he'd been in when they'd gone walking—an event that seemed like another life to Ash now—including the black North Face fleece she'd bought him two Christmases ago. His bare legs, usually one of his most attractive features, had gone a strange grey colour.

She tried to whisper his name but all that came out was a toad-like croak. Tears stung her eyes. She had to hold him one last time, even if it was the last thing she ever did. But as she moved to go towards him, she looked down and saw that she was standing on a chair. If she stepped off it, the rope would tighten and she'd be left hanging in mid-air.

She grabbed at the noose, hunting for the knot with shaking, fumbling fingers.

'Don't bother, my love. I'm right behind you. All I have to do is give that chair a little kick and you'll be throttled like one of last year's chickens.'

Ash froze, wondering what new nightmare was in store for her as Dora walked into view, stopping in front of her. Ash could have kicked the old lady full in the face, but to do so risked knocking herself off the chair and she could see that Dora knew that. The old lady was giving her one of her friendly smiles, but there was a cruel twinkle in her eye. It made Ash think of nasty little boys pulling the legs off spiders.

'What's going on?' Ash asked her, the words coming out in a thick slur.

'I was waiting for you to wake up, my love. You see, I want to watch you suffer after what you did to my Stuart. I don't want you to die peacefully in your sleep. I want to see you dangle and kick. I want to see your face change colour while the life chokes out of you.'

She stepped forward, a foot touching one of the chair legs, looking up at Ash as she did so, lapping up her fear. She was still wearing the same dress and pinafore, her hair in the same bun. Even now Ash found it hard to grasp that this old lady in front of her was just about to end her life.

'Why?' she whispered.

'I told you. You killed my youngest child. Beat him like an animal. You're going to have to pay for that.'

'We just tried to help the girl.' Ash was finding her voice again now. 'That's all we did. Who was she?'

Something crossed the old lady's features then. Was it regret? 'She's just one of many,' she answered with a sigh.

'But why do you do it?' Suddenly Ash had to know, even though she knew it would do no good. 'Why do you kidnap girls?'

'I don't, my love. They're nothing to do with me. My sons just look after them, and make sure they don't escape. Which this time they didn't do a very good job of. The girls belong to the man who owns the estate—the banker from London. He likes to have his way with them. You know what men are like. But some men are worse than others. And our lord of the manor has some strange tastes. He has his way with the girls, and when he's finished with them, my boys clean up the mess.'

'Oh God.'

'I'm afraid God doesn't spend time up in these parts, my love. It's the Devil's work that we do here. It's not nice. Not for any of us. But needs must when he comes calling. And the lord pays us very well. Very well indeed. It was just unfortunate that you got caught up in it. A case of the wrong place at the wrong time, I'm afraid. That was Stuart's fault. The girl should never have got away. The problem was, as soon as she ran into you, you all had to die. There is no way we can afford to let the secret of the manor get out, and have the police sniffing round here. We're all too involved for that. Stuart's paid the price for his mistake. And now it's your turn.'

Ash didn't know what to say. It was almost impossible to believe there were people out there who could murder young women for pleasure, and others who protected their secrets for money. Maybe it happened far more than she was aware of. After all, Ash had led a sheltered, middle-class life. She knew nothing of the grim lives of the thousands of young foreign women in the country. Many of them were probably disappearing every day with no one to notice their absence.

'What's the matter, my love? Cat got your tongue?'

'You'll never get away with this,' Ash told her, desperately hoping she was right. Someone had to be punished for this atrocity. For the murder of her beloved husband, for the murders of Guy and Tracy, for all the other unsolved killings. And for the murder of Ash herself, because right then she knew that she was going to die.

Dora smiled. 'Oh, we will get away with it, my love. Don't you worry your pretty little head about that.'

'No one will believe you.'

'Well, that's our lookout, isn't it? You should consider yourself lucky, my love. We were going to take you up to the estate to replace the girl who escaped, and let the lord have his way with you. That would have been a lot worse than this, I promise you. Rory and Stuart have told me what those girls look like after the lord has finished with them. I have to say, it makes very unpleasant listening.'

She looked up at Ash, a mocking smile on her fat face. 'But we thought it would be easier this way. Girl drinks too much. Girl goes mad with a knife. Girl kills her husband and friends. Girl hangs herself in shame. Hard to explain why something like that would happen, of course, but then . . . ' She shrugged, kicking the chair and sending it flying. 'Who can explain such things?'

CHAPTER THIRTEEN

'Messy business this one,' said DCI Duncan Jarrett of Strathclyde CID, stepping out of the lodge and shutting the door behind him. He was keen to escape the stench of death and decay before it became obvious to his colleagues that it was making him feel sick. He took a deep breath, savouring the fresh forest air, and turned to DS Jimmy Gray, who'd been in charge of securing the scene. 'Those bodies must have been in there for days.'

'Four of them, according to the coroner,' said Gray, scratching at his belly through his shirt.

'And no one reported them

missing? What is it with these English?'

Gray shrugged. 'One of the couples was from Singapore, and were here on their holidays, so no one noticed they'd gone. The other couple was from London, and you know what they're like down there. They all ignore each other. It was only the woman's school that finally raised the alarm after she hadn't turned up at work for three days.'

'Anyone got any idea what happened?'

'Looks like they had some sort of argument, and the woman, Ashleigh Murray, attacked the others. Her fingerprints are all over the murder weapon.' He stopped itching his belly, leaving his shirt partly untucked. A small roll of flabby white flesh stuck out. 'There was a lot of booze in her system, so it looks like she sobered up, had a fit of remorse over what she'd done, and hanged herself.'

'Has she got a record of mental illness?'

Gray shook his head and lit a cigarette. 'Not that we know of.'

The whole thing didn't look right to Jarrett. It wasn't just the fact that a young female teacher of previous good character had knifed her husband and two friends to death. It was the fact that the bodies had been discovered in different parts of the house. Would she really have been able to chase them round with a knife and kill them one by one without being overpowered? If so, why wasn't there blood all over the walls?

These were all questions that were worth asking, but Jarrett knew not to push it too far. Thirty years of working in Glasgow had taught him that even the most ordinary-looking people are capable of the most brutal things. And that the obvious solution to a crime is usually the right one.

He turned to the big uniformed

PC standing a few feet away. 'Bet you've never had one like this on your beat before, have you?'

'Can't say I have, sir,' said PC Rory McLean. 'It scares me, to tell you the truth. My ma lives on her own a couple of miles from here and she's in her seventies. Frightening to think this could happen on her doorstep.'

'Anybody else live round here?'

PC McLean shook his head. He was a big man. His thick, pale arms were covered in highly detailed tattoos. Jarrett thought he'd have made a good rugby player, except for the fact that, with his boyish, pudgy features, he looked soft. 'No. This whole stretch of country's empty. It's what attracts the English. The fact that they're not going to see anyone when they're up here.' He looked towards the lodge. 'So, do you think you're going to be looking for anyone? Do I need to tell Ma to be on her guard?'

McLean looked genuinely

concerned. Jarrett thought it was nice to see a man being so protective of his mother.

The DCI sighed. 'No,' he said, thinking about the pretty young woman hanging from the beam in the living room, and wondering what on earth could have been going through her head, 'I don't think we're looking for anyone else.'

McLean smiled. 'You don't know how much better that makes me feel.'